The Dr. Block Reader
Volume 1

Creeptastic
Diary of a Minecraft Bat
Diary of a Werewolf Steve

By,

If you like this book, **please leave a review where you bought it** so other Minecrafters can learn about it.

Thank you!

Table of Contents

Creeptastic

The diary of a misunderstood creeper
and how he saved Steve's life
(An unofficial Minecraft autobiography)

Chapter 1

My first memory is of darkness. And then, slowly, the world got brighter, or maybe my eyes were just adjusting to the moonlight.

I looked around for a while, trying to see something. The first thing I saw was an ugly green and black thing. When I turned my head, the ugly thing was gone. But then I looked back, and I saw it again.

I soon realized that I was looking into a dark pool of water and that I was looking at my own reflection. And, boy, was I ugly! I was mostly green with gray and white spots here and there. My eyes and mouth were as black as pitch.

It made me very sad to realize that I was so hideous, but I must have been spawned for a reason other than to bring ugliness to the world. I needed to discover what that reason was.

But, how would I find out what my purpose in life was? I had no idea. I decided to start wandering around to see if I could find anything or anyone who could help me.

I walked for a long time in a flat, featureless landscape. I was bored and lonely.

Eventually, I made it to a forest with oak and birch trees. I bumped into an oak tree, and it did not feel good. I hissed at the tree, but the tree did not do anything. I guess my purpose in life was not to hiss at trees.

A few minutes later, I saw eight red eyes glowing inside a nearby cave. I walked over to the cave and saw that the glowing red eyes belonged to a small, young spider with a bluish tint.

I hissed at the cave spider. He hissed back.

I had found my first friend. I was very happy.

"Why do you live in this cave?" I asked the spider.

"Because, I hide from a mysterious figure. If he walks by, I try to jump on him from behind and bite him and kill him."

I was frightened by the spider's evil and vicious desire to kill. "Why do you want to kill the mysterious figure?" I asked.

The spider hissed again. "Because he kills other spiders with his iron sword."

"Maybe it is self-defense," I suggested.

The spider hissed at me and said, "You are stupid and ugly. Go away."

And that is how I lost my first friend.

I was very sad that I was alone again, but the cave spider was mean and I did not like him anymore.

Chapter 2

About an hour after I left the spider's cave, I noticed the world becoming brighter. I had never seen so much light.

As it became brighter, I noticed a glowing square rising in the east. Somehow I knew it was the sun. I was born in darkness. Would I be able to survive in so much light?

But, before I could worry about the light for too long, I saw something so terrifying, I am almost unable to write about it.

I saw a burning zombie. I rushed over to him and tried to push him into a pool of water to put out the flames, but he moaned at me and pushed me away.

"I have to get to the village," he said in a grumbling voice.

"Why?" I asked.

"To eat the villagers," he said with a deep and emotionless voice.

"That is horrible. Why would you want to do that?" I asked.

"Because I am a zombie, you ugly green creeper noob," he said.

"A creeper? I am a creeper?" I said.

The burning zombie stopped walking and looked at me like I was a fool. "Duh, noob. Of course you are a creep—."

But before he could finish, the zombie burst into flames and died, leaving only a small pile of rotten flesh. Gross.

I later learned that zombies die from light exposure and this zombie died because he was talking to me because I was a noob and didn't know anything. I was responsible for this poor creature's death. I felt as sick as my green skin looked.

But, at least I now knew what I was: a creeper. But, I still did not know what my purpose in life was or *why* I felt like I needed to find something or someone to make my life complete.

I decided to go to the village to see if I could talk to anyone there. Maybe they could help me with my quest.

Chapter 3

When I got to the village, I tried to talk to a priest, a blacksmith, and a librarian. But they could not understand my hissing, and I could not understand the strange noises coming from their squishy mouths.

I could tell when the villagers looked at me, they only saw my ugly exterior. They were repulsed and frightened. Even if we could have understood each other, I knew they would not have helped me.

I was about to leave the village when I saw ... him.

I felt drawn to him. I felt like I could not live without being near him. But, I did not know *why* I felt this way.

All I knew was that he was **Steve**.

Don't ask me how I knew his name. It was as if the knowledge was hardwired into my brain when I was spawned, and it just took seeing him for me to remember him.

Steve was trading with a farmer to try and get some emeralds. I noticed the emeralds were green, like me. But, the emeralds were beautiful and I was ugly. Why didn't I shine like a beautiful emerald?

I started to walk toward Steve, like I was being drawn to him by some invisible force. Even if I had wanted to go somewhere else, I could not have resisted the pull of Steve.

Steve looked over at me and I could tell that he was afraid of me. Why? Why would he be afraid of me? I may have been hideously ugly, but I was full of love for Steve.

Steve stuffed his newly-acquired emeralds in his pockets, and started to run away. He could run very fast.

I followed him. I needed to get to him for some reason I still could not understand.

Unfortunately, he was too fast and was soon out of sight. But, I still felt his pull and knew that I would walk for the rest of my life just to get close to him.

"One day, oh Great One," I hissed aloud. "I will get close to you."

Chapter 4

As I left the village, I walked in the direction Steve had gone. I walked as fast as I could, but my four stubby little green legs did not go very fast.

"Curse you, stubby legs," I hissed and wailed aloud.

I was so sad. I had discovered that my purpose in life was to be near Steve, but I still did not know *why* that was my purpose. It did not make any sense. I did not even know Steve, so why would I need to be close to him?

And, even though I would never harm him, Steve ran away from me when he looked at me. It must have been because I was so ugly.

Why was I cursed with this horrible green, blocky body? Why?!?!?

I walked alone for hours. I passed trees and rocks and pools of water and lava, but saw no other creatures.

Suddenly, I heard a rustling sound coming from the bushes next to me. I turned to look at it. Who or what could be in the bushes? Maybe I could meet a new friend? I was so lonely.

But it was not a friend.

Out from the bushes came the most hideous creature I have ever seen. It was even uglier and more terrifying than me. It was a brown spotted creature about two feet tall, with four legs and a long tail. It meowed at me.

I felt true, bone-chilling terror for the first time in my life. It was the opposite of the joy I felt when I first saw Steve. I was terrified to my ugly green core. I turned and ran from the ocelot as quickly as I could.

I could hear the ocelot chasing me. It was much faster than me. It jumped on my blocky green head and sank its claws deep into my green flesh.

"Ahhhhh," I hissed with pain. If I had arms, I could have pushed it off, but I did not. I was helpless against its terrifying attack.

The ocelot meowed and laughed at me. "What are you, foolish creeper, some kind of noob?"

"What do you mean, you hideous beast?" I screamed.

"Don't you know you should stay away from ocelots? That we are the enemies of creepers?" the ocelot said as he let go of my head and jumped to the ground.

"No, I only spawned yesterday. I don't know anything," I cried. I was wishing I had arms to check the scratches on my head.

"That is why you are a noob," said the ocelot, laughing at me as he walked away back to his bush.

Chapter 5

"Why was everyone always calling me a noob?" I hissed aloud as I wandered away from the ocelot's bush. "I spawned last night. I can't learn everything in one day."

I stopped walking and stood still, trying to pick up the location of Steve. I felt a faint sensation that told me the direction to go to find Steve. I started walking towards him.

After I had walked for a few more hours, it was getting dark again. I was not scared of the dark. In fact, I liked the dark because I had been born in the dark and no one could see my ugly green body except other creatures of the night.

When it was pitch black, I heard two creatures yelling at each other nearby.

"No, you are the stupid one."

"I'm not stupid. You are the one who shot yourself with an arrow yesterday."

"I only shot myself because I was trying to shoot you and you were so scared you hid behind a rock and the arrow bounced off the rock and hit me."

"You still shot yourself, noob."

"Don't call me a noob! I spawned three days before you. If anyone is a noob, it's you."

I walked closer to these creatures to get a better look. Because I could see at night, I saw they were skeletons. What a strange world I was born into with zombies and skeletons. Who knows what else lived here?

I walked up to the two skeletons and hissed, "Hello."

They stopped fighting and looked at me. "What do you want, creeper?" said one of them.

"I want to find Steve."

The skeletons laughed. "The only thing you creepers ever want to do is find Steve. You guys are so boring."

"Guys? You mean there are more creepers than just me?" I couldn't believe it. I was not the only hideously ugly green blocky thing alive in the world.

"What are you, some kind of noob?" said one of the skeletons.

"Why does everyone keep calling me a noob?" I asked, hissing and whining at the same time (which is actually pretty hard to do).

"Because you are one. You don't know anything," said the other skeleton.

I was sad because I kept being insulted by everyone I met. I just wanted to learn how this world worked. Why didn't anyone help me? I decided I was not going to let these skeletons insult me. I had had enough!

"I may not know everything," I said. "But I do know one thing."

The skeletons laughed. "Yeah, right. What one thing is that?"

"I know that **Steve is love; Steve is life**," I said with conviction.

The skeletons started laughing so hard, I thought they might fall apart into piles of bones.

"See?" said one skeleton to the other. "He's a total noob. He doesn't even know what creepers are supposed to do to

Steve." And they started laughing even harder.

"What do you mean? What am I supposed to *do* to Steve?" I asked. Finally, I would learn *why* I was drawn so strongly to Steve.

But before they could answer, they actually did fall apart into piles of bones, each with a single arrow on top. They had laughed themselves to pieces and died.

I stood over their piles of bones and shook my head sadly at how the meanness of the skeletons had caused their own demise.

"Who's the noob now?" I hissed.

Chapter 6

I left the skeleton bones and started walking east toward the horizon where the sun was beginning to rise. I sensed Steve was in that general direction.

I walked for hours until the sun was high in the sky. I walked past beautiful red poppies and lovely yellow dandelions. If only I had arms, I would have picked some flowers and smelled them.

I was sad again because the world seemed to be against me. No one liked me, and I was alone. The skeletons had said there were more creepers like me, but I had yet to see any. I thought maybe they were lying to me because they thought I was a noob.

But, then, I heard a familiar hissing sound. In fact, I heard lots of hissing sounds. It sounded like the hissing sound I made.

I forgot about Steve for a moment and walked as quickly as I could toward the hissing sounds. The noise seemed to be coming from the other side of a large blocky boulder.

I walked around the boulder and saw an amazing sight: ten creepers hissing to each other.

"Hi, guys," I hissed excitedly.

"Hi," they all hissed back.

"My name is … uh … well … uh … I … uh … guess I don't have a name," I said sadly.

"What are you, some sort of noob? Creepers don't have names," said one of them.

"We don't?" I asked.

"Of course not," said another.

"Why don't we have names?" I asked.

"I don't know," said a third one. "Creepers just gonna creep, man."

"Gonna creep? What does that mean?" I was so confused.

"We creep until we find Steve."

Suddenly, I became very happy. They were looking for Steve too. Maybe we could find Steve together.

"I saw Steve yesterday," I said excitedly.

They all looked at me with shocked expressions. Their black mouths hanging open. "Where? Where did you see him?" They all asked.

"In a village near the forest, about a day's walk from here."

"We must go there," one said.

"Why?" I asked. "Steve is no longer there. He went to the east, toward the rising sun."

"He did? How do you know?" asked one of the creepers.

"I sense him. I have been following the sensation. Don't you sense him too?" I asked.

"Not unless we are very close. It seems your Steve sensor is very powerful. You should lead us to Steve," one of them suggested.

The happiness inside of me was so powerful, I started to shake. I was shaking faster and faster. Suddenly, I felt very warm.

"Look out," screamed one of the other creepers. "He's going to explode."

My happiness left me and was replaced by an intense fear. I stopped shaking and became very cold. "What do you mean? Explode?"

"Seriously? You don't know?" they asked.

"I didn't know I could explode," I confessed.

"Yes, that is what creepers do. We find Steve and then we explode. But, sometimes we can explode if we get too excited."

"What do you mean, we find Steve and then explode? Why would we do that?" I asked.

"Because, a creeper's purpose in life is to kill Steve," hissed one of the creepers menacingly.

"No!" I screamed. "Steve is love. Steve is life."

"You are a fool," said another creeper. "Why would you think such nonsense?"

"When I saw Steve, I knew he was a great man. I knew that I would do anything for him. I knew that I would follow him forever."

The creepers looked at me like I was not only a noob, but a crazy noob.

"We are sorry you feel that way. But, thank you for telling us where to find Steve. We will take care of him," said another creeper.

"No," I hissed. "I can't let you –."

And then a large block of iron ore landed on my head and knocked me out.

Chapter 7

When I woke up, a wolf was licking my face. I wanted to pet the wolf to thank him for waking me up, but I did not have any arms. So, I just hissed, "Thank you, wolf." The wolf smiled at me and walked away.

I was alone again. But, I was not sad anymore. Instead, I was angry. I had to stop the gang of creeper assassins from killing Steve.

I stood up and felt dizzy. That block of iron ore did not feel very good. I could tell I had a big bump on my head. I could not believe my own kind would push a block of ore onto my head. The thought made me even more determined to stop them.

I looked down and saw the footprints of the creepers heading to the east. I started following them, walking as quickly as I could.

I soon realized that I would never catch up with the creeper assassins just by walking. I had to move more quickly. But how? I couldn't fly. I couldn't swim. I couldn't even run.

I kept walking and thinking about how to go faster.

After an hour, I had followed the tracks of the creeping pack of murderers up a mountain path, but they were still nowhere to be seen.

From my location, I looked down and saw a horse grazing on grass about twenty feet below me at the bottom of a sheer drop. The horse was wearing bronze armor, so it must be tamed.

Horses are fast, I thought. What if I could ride a horse? I had no idea if my plan would work, but I had to try. I had to save Steve.

I walked to the very edge of the mountain and looked down. I lined myself up with the horse's back and then I jumped.

"Ahhhhh," I hissed as I fell through the air.

I landed on the horse with a thud and somehow managed to stay on his back. The horse bucked me a couple of times, and I almost fell off. I was gripping the horse's back with my four stubby legs. I had to stay on. If I fell off, I'd never be able to get back on.

"Stop, horse, you have to help me save Steve," I hissed.

When the horse heard me say "Steve," he stopped trying to buck me off. He turned his head and looked at me.

"You are ugly," he said.

I sighed. "I know. I know. But, will you help me save Steve?"

"I know Steve," said the horse. "He tamed me."

"Why aren't you still with him then?" I asked, amazed and honored to be riding Steve's very own horse.

"We were attacked by a bunch of zombies and Steve told me to run away to save my life," said the horse. "I haven't seen him since then."

"Well, I have seen him, and he is in danger from a gang of creeper assassins.

You must help me save him," I begged the horse.

"But, you are a creeper," said the horse. "Why would you want to save Steve?"

"Because," I said, "Steve is love. Steve is life."

"I believe you, creeper. I believe you because no creeper would ever say that unless he really meant it."

"Thank you, horse," I said. "I would stroke your mane, but I don't have any arms or hands."

"That is okay," said the horse. "I understand."

I looked to the sky and saw the sun was beginning to set. "We don't have much time," I said to the horse. "The creeper gang will catch up to Steve just after dark. He won't stand a chance. We must hurry."

The horse neighed and then galloped toward the east. We soon located the footprints left by the creepers, and the horse followed them as quickly as he could.

I hoped we would not be too late.

Chapter 8

About thirty minutes later, we heard an explosion coming from up ahead.

"Oh no," I said to the horse, "we might be too late."

The horse galloped as fast as he could. When we got close enough, we saw the creeper gang had pushed Steve up the side of a mountain. The creepers were following him up the mountain.

Steve was cornered. The mountain was so steep that Steve could not climb any higher. Soon, one of the creeper assassins was sure to get close enough to blow him up.

Steve was shooting at the creepers with a bow and arrow, but his position on the mountain was so precarious that he had a hard time lining up a good shot. He would not be able to kill them all.

I jumped off the horse and ran over to the creepers.

"Stop it," I hissed. "You have to let Steve live."

"Stand aside, noob," said one of the creepers. "Let the real creepers do what needs to be done."

The creepers walked past me like I wasn't even there. They were starting to form a pyramid, climbing on top of each other to get closer to Steve. It would not be much longer before Steve would be within their blast radius.

I started pacing back and forth. What could I do? How could I save Steve?

I stood at the edge of the mountain and looked down at a pool of lava below. Just then, I had a brilliant idea. If I could somehow push the creepers into the lava, I could kill them and save Steve.

But how?

I asked myself, what would Steve do?

And then, I knew what I had to do.

I had to sacrifice myself to save the great Steve from the creeper horde. Steve needed to live in order to build a bigger and better world out of block-shaped objects, one block at a time.

I walked toward Steve. I felt his power and love flowing through me. I felt so happy that I started to shake even though I was still very far away from Steve. I could feel myself becoming very warm.

One of the other creepers looked at me with horror. "What are you doing?" he hissed.

"I am saving Steve. He is love. He is life," I said.

"No," screamed the creeper. "You wouldn't dare."

But I did dare.

Chapter 9

Hi, guys! This is Steve writing now. I wanted to finish the story of the bravest, most honorable creeper I have ever known.

I watched as the creeper blew himself up in the center of the creeper horde. Some of them died instantly, while others were blown into the lava below and burned to death.

All of the dead creepers, except the brave one, dropped gunpowder. This creeper dropped a diary. By some magical process I don't yet understand, the diary had recorded all of this creeper's thoughts and acts.

You have been reading this same diary. I only wanted to write a few more words in it so you would understand that this amazing creeper's sacrifice was not in vain.

When I read this diary, I was humbled and inspired. To honor this creeper's sacrifice, I will continue to put even greater effort into my mining and crafting work in the Overworld and beyond.

And to any hostile mobs out there who might read this book, I say:

I am still alive.

I am still here.

This is *my* world.

The End

DIARY OF A MINECRAFT BAT

(an unofficial Minecraft autobiography)

Chapter 1

They call me "Swirly," but my real name is Jasper. I am a bat.

I sleep all day and explore the Overworld at night. Most of my friends think I am weird because I like to explore. But, most of my friends are super-boring and only want to fly around looking for things to eat. Unlike them, I crave adventure and knowledge. And, sometimes, you have to seek out both of those things; they don't just find you.

That is actually how I got my nickname. I was exploring the depths of a cave and heard a strange noise. It was a loud rumbling sound, almost like an explosion, but the ground was not shaking and the sound was continuous.

I went deeper and deeper into the cave and found a massive underground waterfall. I flew down the length of the waterfall to the lake into which it fell. I flapped my wings to hover just above the lake. Inside the lake the water was spinning around like a square top.

I stared at the spinning water and was drawn to it like I was hypnotized. Without realizing what was happening, I fell in. I was pushed around and around in the whirlpool, which was not very enjoyable for two reasons. First, I was getting wet. Second, as I spun around, I kept hitting a rock on the edge of the lake.

Fortunately, my friend Arnold was exploring with me. (Arnold is my coolest friend. He thinks I'm a bit weird, but he doesn't mind.) He hovered above me and I was able to grab hold of his feet so he could pull me out.

"Did you enjoy your swirly, Jasper?" he asked, laughing.

"No," I said.

Arnold, of course, had to tell this story to all of our friends, and someone started calling me "Swirly."

"Don't call me Swirly!" I would yell.

Naturally, seeing how much discomfort it caused me, my friends kept calling me Swirly until it became my nickname.

Whatever. I'm used to it now.

I just wish I could convince more of my friends to come on adventures with me and Arnold. They have no idea what awesome things they are missing.

Chapter 2

One night, Arnold and I were out flying around and looking for food. We were making chirping noises as part of our echolocation system. (By the way, it is pretty cool to be able to see using sound. You should try it sometime.)

Anyhow, we had already found a few insects to eat, and we were thinking about looking for an oak tree so we could eat the apples from it. (*Shouldn't it be called an apple tree?*) I prefer fruit to insects any day.

We were flying low above the forest looking for some oak trees with apples. Sometimes, we found fruiting oak trees near farms established by players. It was during our search for fruit that Arnold noticed something.

"Hey, Swirly, look over there," said Arnold, pointing with his wing.

I looked over in the direction Arnold had pointed. I saw an opening to a cave we had never noticed before. "Wow," I said, "I don't think I've ever been inside of that cave."

"Me neither," said Arnold. "Let's check it out."

The two of us flew over to the entrance to the cave. It was three blocks high and two blocks wide and went straight into the mountain for quite some distance.

Because we were nocturnal animals, we could easily see in the dark and had no need for torches in order to explore the cave. (And, even if it had been pitch black, we could have used our echolocation to find our way.)

We flew inside the cave and soon came to a fork in the entry passage. We never like to explore a cave passage alone because it is far too dangerous, so we had to decide which passage to take. Whenever we had to make a decision about exploration, we made that decision playing Rock, Paper, Scissors. Whoever won the game, would choose the passage.

"One. Two. Three. Shoot!" I said. I stuck out my wing, holding it flat like a piece of paper. At the same time, Arnold put out his wing, with the points of his claw separated like pair of scissors. He won.

Arnold decided we should go down the passageway on the left. As we went deeper and deeper into the passage, it was clear that the passage had been formed naturally. It was not a mine. If it had been, I would have been on alert for TNT traps or even players who were mining.

We could hear the flow of water somewhere within the passage. Occasionally, we noticed gleaming ore in the walls.

"That looks like redstone ore," said Arnold.

"It sure does," I said. "I bet some of those players who like to mine the Overworld would be really happy to find this place."

After walking for about ten minutes, we came to a portion of the passageway that descended very rapidly. We followed the passageway down until it opened into another large chamber. It was probably ten blocks by fifteen blocks with irregular edges, just as a natural chamber should be.

In the center of the chamber was a small pool of lava, which cast a bright orange glow against the walls of the chamber. I could see various types of ore in the wall reflecting the glow of the lava.

As we stood there staring at the glinting reflections inside the chamber, we heard a clicking noise.

"Sounds like a spider," said Arnold.

I wasn't quite sure that was what it sounded like. "Well, if it is a spider, it sounds like a really big spider."

Arnold shrugged. "Maybe it's the bunch of spiders."

Arnold was not too concerned, and neither was I. Spiders and bats get along fairly well. We are all predominantly cave dwellers and both species like to eat insects. So, we actually have a lot in common.

After a moment, though, I saw what was making the noise, and it was not a spider.

Chapter 3

I tapped Arnold on the shoulder to draw his attention away from the glow of the lava pool. When he looked at me, I pointed and said, "Dude, that is not a spider."

Arnold looked over where I was pointing and, after his eyes nearly popped out of his head, he said, "Holy bits and pieces, Swirly. What *is* that thing?!?"

Before us stood a horse, but it was not a regular horse. Instead, it was made entirely of bones. It was a skeleton horse, and it was coming right towards us.

"What ... what ... what are you?" I stammered.

The horse looked at us and tilted its skull back and forth, like it was sizing us up. I wasn't sure if he was thinking about eating us or attacking us or just walking away. All I knew was that this horse was very creepy.

"I'm a skeleton horse," said the skeleton horse.

"Yes, I could tell you were the skeleton *of* a horse," I said. "But how did you become a skeleton horse?"

The horse shook its neck back and forth as if to flip its mane, but because it was just bones it made a spooky crackling noise instead. Then the horse said, "I have always been a skeleton horse. I was spawned this way."

It was then that I remembered I had once heard a rumor about the existence of skeleton horses. One of the wise old bats who lived in my cave had told me that he had seen skeleton horses wandering in the Overworld many years ago. However, he had not seen one in a long time and had heard that for whatever reason, they no longer spawned in the Overworld.

"How old are you?" I asked.

"I do not know," said the horse. "I just know that one day I was walking in the forest and the next moment I was inside this cave. I have not been able to find my way out of the cave since."

"That's really strange," I said. "Were you teleported to the cave or something?"

"I don't know how I got here," said the horse. "It was almost instantaneous. It was as if someone decided to remove me from the Overworld and instead of killing me or despawning me, that same someone put me somewhere from which I could never escape or bother anyone."

I shook my head sadly and said, "Gee, that doesn't sound like much fun."

The horse looked at me with its empty eye sockets. I don't know how I could tell, but I felt as though the horse was almost crying. "Yes," said the horse, "it was not a very nice thing to do. I have been lonely for a long time."

"Why don't you come with us?" said Arnold. "We know how to get out of here."

The horse hesitated. "I don't know if that would be such a good idea," said the horse. "A power greater than me and greater than both of you put me in this cave for a reason. I think I should stay here."

"That's ridiculous," I said. "You shouldn't let some invisible force control what you do and who you are. I think you should come with us."

The horse stood there for a moment, contemplating our offer. He had no expression on his face other than the creepy grin of bright white teeth in his skull, but I could tell he was considering the proposal. He shook the bones that would've been his tail and flipped his head back and forth as he thought.

Finally, the horse said, "I appreciate your offer, but I think I will stay here in the cave. If I knew there were more horses like me, I might leave the cave to visit with them, but I fear that I may be the last skeleton horse living in the

Overworld. I would rather be here by myself."

I had to respect the horse's wishes, though I had hoped he would come with us. "I understand," I said. "Arnold and I will come back and visit you in a few days so that you can have someone to talk to."

"We will?" said Arnold, somewhat surprised.

I elbowed Arnold with one of my wings. "Of course we will, you jerk. We have to talk to skeleton horse so that he will not be so lonely."

"Okay, I guess that would be a good thing to do," said Arnold.

The skeleton horse reared up on its hind legs and let out a strange neighing that sounded like a combination between a whistle and a rock grinder. When his feet returned to the ground, he said,

"That sounds great, bats. By the way, what are your names?"

We introduced ourselves as Arnold and Jasper, though of course Arnold had to tell the skeleton horse that my nickname was Swirly.

"My nickname used to be Bones," said the skeleton horse. "But my real name is Domino."

"Nice to meet you, Domino," I said.

"Hey, Swirly, we probably should get going back to our own cave," said Arnold. "I think it will be daylight soon and we should get some sleep."

"Yeah, I think you're right," I replied.

I looked over at Domino who was standing in the corner of the chamber.

"Okay, Domino," I said, "we will be back in a few days to talk to you and tell you about our adventures."

"That would be great," said Domino. "Goodbye."

Chapter 4

A few nights later, I was playing games with some of my bat friends, including Arnold. We were playing hide-and-go-seek, capture the apple, and dive bomb. We were having a lot of fun.

One of my friends named Markus pointed to a far away hill with his wing and said, "Let's see who can fly to the top of that hill the fastest."

"Okay," we all said.

"On your mark. Get set. Go!" shouted Markus.

We took to the air and flew as fast as we could. I tried hard, but could never win these speed games. I got there fifth out of six bats.

When I landed, I was breathing hard. I leaned forward and put the tips of my wings on my scrawny knees while I caught my breath. "Wow," I said, "that was tough. Who won?"

I did not get any response. I stood up and said, "Uh, guys, who won?"

"Who cares," said Markus. "Look."

I looked and saw something I had never seen before. It was a large black rectangle made from what appeared to be obsidian. Inside the black rock rectangle a strange glowing purple substance, rippling with the spinning of many vortexes.

"What is that?" I asked, completely amazed by what I was seeing.

"We thought you might know," said Arnold. "You're the one always talking to the old bats in our cave."

I shook my head. "No one has ever mentioned a glowing purple box before."

"Maybe it's some weird art project," suggested my friend, Flea. (His real name was John, but he was very small for his age so we called him Flea. I guess it wasn't a very nice nickname, but neither is Swirly.)

"That's ridiculous, Flea," said Arnold. "Who would make an art project out here?"

Flea shrugged. "Maybe a player would."

"Hmmm," muttered Arnold as he considered Flea's words. "Actually, you might have something there, Flea. Players are always doing weird stuff."

"What do you think that purple stuff is?" I asked. "It looks like it might be soft."

"Let's find out," said Arnold as he bent down and picked up a rock. "Here it goes," he said as he tossed the rock into the purple stuff.

We watched in amazement as the rock went right through the purple. "Let's try that again," I said, walking behind the rectangle to retrieve the rock. But, there was no rock.

"Hey, Arnold," I said.

"What?"

"Pick up another rock and toss it through the purple stuff. I want to see where it lands this time."

"Ok," said Arnold, as he picked up another rock and tossed it through the rectangle. But, the rock did not go through the rectangle, it disappeared inside of it.

"Whaaa?" I said, amazed. "The rock disappeared."

"I don't like this," said Flea.

"Do you know what this means?" I said. "It means that this rectangle might be a portal to another dimension." I had always wanted to discover another dimension. This might be my chance.

"Yeah, right," said Markus. "Prove it."

"Okay," I said. "Come over here and stand on this side of the portal." Markus came over and stood by me.

"Now, stay there and I'll go around the other side and stick my wing into the portal. If it is just a thin purple thingy, my wing should stick out the other side, right?"

Markus shrugged. "I suppose."

I walked around and put my wing into the purple. The tip of my wing began to feel warm. Not hot, just warm. "So?" I asked.

"Dude, I don't see anything," said Markus. "That's insane."

"I think we should see what's on the other side of this portal," I said.

"No way." "Nope." "Forget it." "You are crazy."

"Yeah, let's do it," said Arnold. I knew I could count on Arnold for an adventure.

"Okay, you wimpy bats. Me and Arnold are going to see what this other dimension is like. You wait here," I said. "If we aren't back in an hour, go tell one of the old bats what happened."

They all nodded.

I looked at Arnold. "Ready?"

"Let's do this."

And, we leapt into the void.

Chapter 5

After we jumped, things were black for a moment, and then we emerged into a strange region.

"It's pretty warm in here, isn't it, Swirly?" said Arnold.

"Yeah, and look at the strange orange and red glow everything has," I said.

We looked behind us and saw the portal. "I guess we can get back to the guys if we go through that," I said.

"Probably," said Arnold. "Come on. Let's look around."

We did not want to risk flying in this strange dimension, so we walked. We walked slowly and quietly, not knowing what hazards might be waiting for us.

We soon realized why this place was so warm and why everything had a red-orange glow. There was lava everywhere. Pools of it. Streams of it. It was crazy.

"Arnold, it feels like we are inside the ground," I said.

Arnold nodded. "Yeah, maybe we aren't really in another dimension. Maybe it's just hundreds of blocks below the surface of the Overworld."

As we pondered our galactic coordinates, we walked around a corner and saw a horde of zombies. Or, they looked sort of like zombies. As we got closer, we realized it was about twenty zombie pigmen.

"Whoa," said Arnold. "I've never seen so many zombie pigmen in one place!"

I've always liked zombie pigmen. They are not as aggressive as zombies, and they are usually willing to spend some time talking to you since they aren't in a hurry to find a villager to kill.

"Hi, guys," I said as we walked up to the horde.

They all looked at us, and then one of them said, "What are you?"

"We're bats."

"What is a bat?" said another of the pigmen.

"You don't have bats down here?" asked Arnold.

"What do you mean, down here?" asked a pigman. "Here is simply here. No down. No up."

"Let me guess," I said, "you don't travel often?" I probably should not have been making fun of the zombie pigman, but I could not help myself.

"What does travel mean?" asked the pigman.

"Derp," I said as I slapped my forehead with my wing. "Never mind."

Arnold and I left the zombie pigmen to their aimless wandering. They were not as fun to talk to as the zombie pigmen in the Overworld. At least those in the Overworld knew what traveling was. Sheesh!

Chapter 6

We soon noticed another strange creature of this region. It looked like a large floating white cube with tentacles hanging on the underside of its body. When we first noticed this strange creature, it was floating aimlessly with its eyes and mouth closed.

"It must be asleep," I whispered to Arnold."

"Probably. Should we wake it up?" he asked.

"I'm wide awake," said the creature, startling us with its high-pitched whine.

"Sorry. We've never been ... well ... here, so we don't know what lives here," I said.

"You have never been to the Nether?" asked the strange cube.

"Is that where we are?" I asked.

"Yes, of course," said the creature, annoyed at our ignorance.

"I've never heard of the Nether," said Arnold.

"I haven't either," I said.

The creature let out a high-pitched sound, like a meowing cat. I think it was laughing at us. "How sad," said the creature. "The Nether is a wonderful place."

I was not sure I could believe this creature. The Nether certainly was a *different* place, but I would not have used the word "wonderful" to describe it.

"So, what are you?" I asked.

"I am a ghast," it said.

"Aghast at what?" Arnold asked.

"No, you idiot. I am *a* ghast," said the ghast.

"Ohhhh," said Arnold. "It's just that I noticed the tracks of your tears on your face and thought maybe you had been aghast at something and had been crying."

"Leave my presence," said the now angry ghast, "or else I will spit a fireball at you!"

"Let's get out of here," I said to Arnold as I grabbed his wing. We took to the air and flew for a minute, leaving the ghast far behind.

When we landed, Arnold said, "That ghast thing had no sense of humor."

"Why don't you let me do the talking the next time we meet a mysterious creature, okay?" I said.

Arnold crossed his wings defensively. "Okay. Whatever."

I shook my head. I did not like bickering with my friend, but this Nether place was obviously not entirely safe. I've always been better at understanding strange creatures, so I had to take the lead.

"Come on, Arnold. Let's keep exploring."

Chapter 7

We had not gone far when Arnold spotted something weird. It looked like a dark red and black cube, but it was bouncing up and down.

"Do you think it is some sort of weird mineral?" I suggested.

"Could be," said Arnold. "But, even in this strange place, I can't imagine there would be a bouncing rock."

"But if it is a bouncing rock, we can re-write the laws of physics," I said, suddenly very excited.

Arnold looked at me with his you-are-such-a-nerd look and said sarcastically, "Yeah, dude, we *totally* could."

I punched him in the wing. "Let's take a closer look."

We walked slowly over to the dark, bouncing black cube. As we approached, the cube suddenly turned around and we saw that it had red, orange and yellow eyes.

I was so shocked that I yelled, "It's alive!"

"Of course I am alive," said the creature with a gravelly voice.

"We thought maybe you were a bouncing rock," I said.

"Well," said the creature, "that is partly correct. I am a magma cube. So I am a bouncing liquid rock."

"How do you hold your cube shape then?" asked Arnold, already breaking our deal that I do the talking.

"I don't know," said the magma cube. "Why do you have wings?"

"I don't know," said Arnold. "Good point, cube."

"So, do you have a name?" I asked.

"No," said the magma cube.

"Oh," I said. "Well, what do you do all day?"

"I bounce. And, if I see a player, I attack him or her," said the cube.

"Why?" asked Arnold.

"I don't know," said the magma cube. "Why do you ask so many questions?"

"I don't know," said Arnold. "Good point."

I could tell we were not going to get anywhere with this magma cube philosopher, so I said, "Well, we need to be on our way. Good-bye, magma cube."

"Where are you going?" asked the magma cube.

"I think we will go in that direction," I said, pointing.

"Be careful," said the magma cube. "A fearsome creature awaits in that direction."

"Is it dangerous?" asked Arnold, his voice betraying fear.

"Very," said the magma cube. "But, what is worse is its horrific appearance."

"What does it look like?" I asked, scared and excited at the same time. *Adventure and knowledge, here we come!*

"It is too horrible to describe," said the magma cube. "Now, go away."

I was disappointed that the magma cube would not tell us more about this allegedly fearsome creature. But, it was seeming more and more like the inhabitants of the Nether were very inhospitable.

Arnold and I left the magma cube to its bouncing and went off to find the fearsome creature.

Chapter 8

In light of the magma cube's warning, what had started as a sightseeing tour of the Nether had now become a mission of discovery and survival. We jumped at every little sound and shadow. We thought we saw monsters where there were none.

We noticed that the high-pitched wails of the ghasts echoed in this area. There must have been many of them around, but we did not see any.

"Where are all the ghasts hiding?" I asked.

Arnold shrugged. "Maybe they are staying away from the fearsome creature?"

I shivered. "What do you think this creature is?"

"I have a lot of scary ideas, but I think we should not let our imaginations go crazy here," said Arnold. "So far, we've met some freaks in the Nether, but no one I would call 'fearsome'."

"Maybe you are right," I said, feeling a bit more relaxed.

"Yeah," said Arnold, "that magma cube was probably just a wimp."

A few minutes later, we beheld an unexpected sight. Someone or something had created a small opening in a wall. Minecart tracks started just outside the opening and went inside.

"Let's check it out," I said. Arnold agreed and we ducked inside the opening.

The landscape on the other side of the wall looked exactly like the rest of the Nether. The only obvious difference were the minecart tracks extending into the distance, and then curving around a small hill.

We followed the tracks, assuming they would lead to something of interest. When we got around the curve in the tracks, we saw they ended at a wall. It was as if someone had built the wall directly on top of the tracks.

"Dead end," said Arnold.

"Yep," I said. "I guess we should go back."

Arnold started tapping me excitedly on the shoulder. "Dude, look at that," he said, pointing. I saw a shiny rectangular object a few blocks to the left of where the wall covered the tracks.

"Is that made of diamonds?" I asked.

Arnold rushed over to the object and pushed it upright. "Holy extravagant lifestyle, Swirly. It's a diamond minecart!"

"What? What would you need a diamond minecart for?"

"I don't know, dude," said Arnold. "Wait until we tell the guys about this. They'll never believe it."

After trying unsuccessfully to break a few pieces of diamond from the minecart, we turned around and started to follow the tracks back to the opening.

"Gee, Arnold, there must be something important in here for someone to lay all that track and build a diamond minecart," I said.

"Yeah, I wish we could figure out what it is," said Arnold. "Who knows, maybe the fearsome creature lives in here."

As we walked, I scanned the area for any clues, but I saw nothing. When we got to the opening back to the rest of the Nether, I turned around and scanned the area one last time. That was when I saw it.

"Arnold, look," I said. "Up there, on top of that terraced slope."

Arnold squinted in the direction I was pointing. "Is that what I think it is?"

"A cage."

Chapter 9

We walked over to the base of the terraced slope. We could have flown to the top quickly, but we wanted to be careful with our approach, so we hopped quietly up each level of the slope.

As we moved up the slope, we got a better view of the cage. It looked huge, at least twenty blocks long on the side facing us. It appeared to be made out of some dark black blocks.

When we got to the final level before the top, I put my wing on Arnold's shoulder to stop him from going further.

"Arnold," I whispered. "We do not know what is in that cage, so let's just peek over the edge before we rush up there."

"Agreed," said Arnold.

We both slowly raised our heads over the final layer to look at the cage. When we did, I could not believe what we were seeing.

"Kismet," said Arnold.

"What?"

"Destiny. Fate."

He was right. What we saw near the back of the cage, about twenty blocks away, was a skeleton horse.

We stood up and climbed to the final level and stood at the edge of the cage. The horse did not notice us. It was standing with its head down. It looked sad.

"Horse," I shouted. "Horse! Over here!"

The skeleton horse slowly raised its head and then turned to look at us. The horse neighed, sounding just like Domino's neigh – like a combination between a whistle and a rock grinder. It walked over to us slowly.

"I never thought I'd see two bats down here. Who are you?" it asked.

"Jasper and Arnold," I said. "What is your name?"

"My name is Quick."

"Really?" asked Arnold.

"Yes," said Quick. "When I was tamed, the player who tamed me named me Quick."

"Did the player put you here?"

"No, I do not know how I got here. One day I was grazing in the Overworld, and the next, I was here," said Quick.

"Do you know Domino?" I asked.

Quick neighed excitedly. "Yes, we were friends in the Overworld. He had also been tamed by the same player. How can you know Domino?"

"We found him in a cave in the Overworld a few days ago," said Arnold.

"Oh, how I would love to see him again," said Quick, mournfully. "But, I cannot get out of this prison."

"There must be a way you can get out," said Arnold.

"I have already tried everything I can think of. The cage is too strong to break with my hooves, and I cannot dig into the ground," said Quick. "I am trapped forever."

In that moment, I was struck with a sudden inspiration. "Oh my gosh, I think I might be able to get you out," I said.

"How?" asked Arnold.

Instead of answering, I took off and flew back to where we had found the diamond minecart. I searched the area, hoping I could find it. *If they abandoned a minecart, they must have also left behind a ....*

"Yes!" I shouted aloud.

There, resting on the ground behind a pile of rocks was a pickaxe. I grabbed the pickaxe and flew back to the cage.

Chapter 10

It did not take long to free Quick. I just picked away at the netherrack underneath the cage until there was an opening large enough for him to fit through.

Arnold and I cheered as he burst forth from his prison, rearing up and neighing several times, before trotting down the terraced slope. When he got to the bottom of the slope, he ran back and forth testing the strength of his boney legs.

Once Quick had calmed down some, he said, "How do we get to Domino?"

"We have to walk back to the portal that brought us to the Nether," I said.

"Will we have to pass by the creatures of the Nether?" Quick asked wearily.

"Probably," I said. "We talked to some of them on the way here."

"I was afraid of that," said Quick. "They don't like me very much."

"Why?" asked Arnold.

"They think I am some sort of evil creature, put in the cage by some strange force," said Quick. "They call me the 'fearsome creature'."

Arnold laughed, slapping his sides with his wings. "Really? *You* are the fearsome creature?"

"Yes," said Quick as he hung his head. "Sometimes, the Nether mobs walk up to my cage and throw rocks at me. It is mean."

"Wow," I said. "That's terrible."

"Yeah, it was," said Quick. "But, now I am free, thanks to you two. Just get me out of here."

"Let's go," said Arnold. "And if anyone tries to throw a rock at you, they will have to answer to me!"

"Calm down, tough guy," I said. "Let's just get out of here with no hassle and get back to our friends in the Overworld."

We walked to the portal, retracing our steps.

When we saw the bouncing magma cube, the cube screamed and then bounced himself into a pool of lava and swam across to the other side. Once he was safe, he yelled, "Look out, bats, the fearsome creature is right next to you!"

"Duh," said Arnold.

"He's cool, cube," I said.

"He is not cool," wailed the magma cube. "He is fearsome and evil."

"Whatever," I said.

We continued to walk, leaving the magma cube quivering in its corner.

After a few more minutes, we came to the ghast. He was floating above a burning block of netherrack as we approached. He was meowing like a cat who had just inhaled some helium from a birthday balloon.

"Hey, ghast, what's up?" said Arnold.

The ghast opened his eyes and emitted a high-pitched scream. He looked directly at the skeleton horse and spit a fireball at him.

"Great balls of fire, Swirly," said Arnold. "Let's get out of here!"

The three of us ran away as quickly as we could, the ghast in hot pursuit, spitting fireballs at us.

"Quick," I said to the horse, "run as fast as you can. Me and Arnold can fly just in front of you and lead the way."

Quick neighed his agreement with the plan and started running. Quick was true to his name and could run very fast, almost as fast and Arnold and I could fly.

Soon, the ghast had given up the case, and we were able to slow down and catch our breath.

"These Nether creatures really do fear you, Quick," I said. "It's crazy."

"Dude," said Arnold, pointing. "Look!"

Up ahead we could see the portal to the Overworld, just beyond the horde of twenty zombie pigmen.

"That's a lot of pigmen," said Quick. "They *really* don't like me."

Just as he said that, one of the pigmen noticed Quick and said, "It is the fearsome creature. Attack!"

"Just great," I said.

Quick was looking from side to side, trying to find an escape route. "I have a plan," he said. "You guys fly to the portal and I'll catch up."

"No," said Arnold, "we can't leave you here."

"Trust me," said Quick.

"Come on, Arnold. Let's go," I said.

Arnold reluctantly took flight, and I was right behind him. We flew over the horde of zombie pigmen, who did not even glance in our direction. They were fixated on Quick.

We landed on top of the portal and watched. We noticed that Quick was running back in the direction we had come.

"What is he doing?" asked Arnold.

"I don't know," I said.

As the horde of pigmen approached him, Quick suddenly turned around and ran towards them at full speed.

"He's insane," said Arnold. "He's going to try to run through them."

It looked like Arnold was right, but I hoped he was not. I don't think even a super-fast horse like Quick could make it through a horde of pigmen.

Quick was approaching with blazing speed as the pigmen closed in on him. Just as it looked like he was going to be smothered by the pigmen, Quick leapt from the ground and started running on top of the heads of the pigmen!

"Holy migraine headache, Swirly," said Arnold. "Look at that!"

I watched as Quick danced across the heads of the pigmen. With each stride, he came closer to safety. With each stride, a pigman fell under his speedy hooves.

Finally, Quick got to the end of the horde of pigmen and jumped to the ground. Arnold and I cheered and yelled, "Awesome!"

"Piece of cake," said Quick. "Let's get out of here."

We turned and jumped into the portal, ready to leave the Nether behind.

Chapter 11

When we arrived back in the Overworld, I admit I was relieved. Our friends were waiting there for us, along with one of the old bats from our cave. Our friends cheered and were rushing forward to greet us just as Quick emerged from the portal.

"AHHHHHH!!!!! What is that?!?" they shouted.

"That's our friend, Quick," said Arnold. "He is a skeleton horse."

The old bat walked slowly forward and pet the skeleton horse's rib cage. "Wow," said the old bat. "I have not seen one of these mobs since I was a wee child. I thought they had gone extinct."

"Not extinct," I said. "In fact, we are taking him to meet his friend, Domino."

"Who is Domino?" asked the old bat.

"Another skeleton horse we found in a cave a couple days ago," said Arnold. "We were keeping it a secret."

"Amazing," said the old bat. "You kids sure have some astounding adventures."

As we led Quick to the cave to meet Domino, we told our friends and the old bat all about our adventures in the Nether.

"I am never, ever, ever going to the Nether," said Flea.

"Probably a good idea," I said.

***

When we got to Domino's cave, Arnold and I led Quick inside.

"It will only take a few minutes to get to Domino's chamber," I told Quick.

When we got there, Quick neighed to announce his arrival and Domino galloped over to us as quickly as he could.

"Quick? Quick is that you?" asked Domino.

"Yes, my old friend, it is," said Quick.

The two horses moved forward and reared up. They moved their hooves up and down at each other in greeting.

"It's like a horse bro hug," said Arnold, tears forming in his eyes.

After a moment, Quick and Domino came over to us.

"Thank you for finding my friend," said Domino. "I wasn't sure you would even come back, but you did and you came with Quick. Thank you."

"You are welcome," I said.

"Yes," said Quick. "We're reunited and it feels so good."

"Uh, oh ... kay ....," I said. *Weird.*

After that, we led Domino and Quick to the mouth of the cave. It was still dark outside, so they told us they would wait for the sun to come up before they ventured outside to run on the grass.

Arnold and I said goodbye to the horses and told them to visit our cave anytime they wanted to.

Then we went home to our cave and fell into a deep sleep.

The End

DIARY of a
Werewolf Steve

(an unofficial Minecraft autobiography)

Introduction

My name is Steve. Or, at least, it usually is.

What do I mean by that?

Well, it all started with Herobrine.

This should come as no surprise. But, how exactly he forced this horrific change upon me is something that I shudder to tell. It is terrifying.

I feel, however, I must record this tale in my diary so that other players can protect themselves from his wickedness. If I die, I hope that my diary will be found so that others can avoid my fate.

It is a fate I would not wish upon my worst enemy.

Even Herobrine.

Chapter 1

I was minding my own business, doing what I do. I was farming wheat and raising pigs. Just trying to feed myself and stay alive when the hostile mobs attacked.

It was difficult, but enjoyable work. It was, however, lonely work. I needed a companion. And so, I decided to set out to find an ocelot or a wolf to tame for a pet.

In retrospect, I wish I could simply have endured the loneliness.

At least I had my basic needs taken care of. At least I had a home to protect me from the nighttime monsters. At least I could control myself during ....

Anyhow, early one morning, I woke up and stuffed a bunch of fish and bones into my inventory and set out to find a new pet.

I had been mining only for a few days, so the only armor I had was made of leather. But, I had managed to forge an iron sword, so I felt somewhat safe. I figured an iron sword would be enough to protect me during the day. And, if I were attacked, I could probably run back to my house and hide if necessary.

I walked through the nearby forest, hoping to find a companion sooner rather than later.

As I was walking by some bushes, I heard a meowing sound. An ocelot!

I pulled some fish out of my bag and said, "Here, kitty kitty. Here, kitty kitty."

Slowly, the cautious ocelot crept from underneath the bush. Although he was wild, he could not resist the smell of the fish. I tossed one to him, and he ate it quickly. I tossed another, and he gobbled it down. I tossed a third, and he pounced on it, devouring it with amazing speed.

I thought he might be tame enough for me to grab, and so I lunged at him to pick him up. But, I had miscalculated and he scratched my leg. It was a deep cut and bled a lot.

"Ouch! You stupid ocelot," I said. "I just want to be your friend."

The ocelot looked at me and hissed before running away into the mountains.

"Lame," I said aloud as I put a bandage on the scratch to stop it from bleeding.

After patching myself up, I checked my inventory. Only two fish left. There was no way I could tame an ocelot with only two raw fish.

"I guess I'll have to find a wolf to tame," I said, looking at the pile of bones in my inventory.

Having a dog is probably better than having a cat anyway, I thought. *Dogs will help you fight. Cats just run and hide.*

And so, I began looking for a wolf to tame. The problem with taming a wolf is that they can be much more vicious that an ocelot. A bite from a wolf would make the scratch from the ocelot look like a papercut.

I needed to be careful.

Chapter 2

I continued to walk through the forest looking for a wolf. There were no signs of wolves, not even any piles of wolf droppings. I had no clues.

As I walked, I kept my sword at the ready for any hostile mobs who might attack. I was still learning how to be a good warrior, so I was not as confident as the more experienced players I had met while trading in the local village.

I had just turned around the bend in the path when I noticed something odd: a tree with no leaves on it. I had never seen anything like it.

As the wind moved through the barren branches of the tree, the tree swayed back and forth silently, like a hanging skeleton.

Even though it gave me the creeps, I moved closer to the tree. *How did it have no leaves? It did not appear to be dead.*

I walked up to the tree and slashed it with my sword. But, instead of wood chips, it began to ooze a red fluid that looked suspiciously like blood.

What?

Before I could recover from the shock of a bleeding tree, I felt the hair on the back of my neck stand up. Someone or something was watching me.

I slowly turned around. I scanned the forest and the dark crevices in the nearby hill. I saw no movement. It was eerily silent.

And, then, I saw it for the briefest of instants. I thought I saw two glowing white dots, maybe eyes, peeking out at me from a black crack in the hill.

"Who's there?" I shouted.

No response. I could no longer see the white dots, so I cautiously approached the black crack where they had been.

As I got closer, the light from the sun was just strong enough to see all the way to the back of the crack. Nothing.

What or who had I seen?

I did not have much time to ponder this thought because when I turned around, I was faced with a huge, snarling wolf. He stared at me with evil yellow eyes, and he was already starting to drool, anticipating his next meal. Me!

Chapter 3

I knew there was no way that I could defeat this huge wolf with my leather armor and iron sword. He would tear me to shreds before I'd inflicted any type of meaningful damage.

I was preparing to die, hoping to respawn in a better place, when I suddenly got an idea.

I reached into my inventory and threw the six bones that I had at the wolf. The wolf took his eyes off me and started chewing on the bones.

While the wolf was distracted, I ran as fast as I could back toward my house. I knew that if I could get inside the house and lock the door, I would be safe from the wolf.

I turned and ran.

When I had gone about one hundred feet, I looked back. The wolf was still chomping at the pile of bones. Incredibly, he did not seem to be paying attention to me. Maybe he *would* forget about me?

Not exactly.

The wolf was chewing on two bones at once when he suddenly looked up. He stared right at me with his evil yellow eyes and then he let out a murderous howl and started running after me.

I turned and ran.

As I ran, I dropped everything I had except my sword in the hope that I could outrun him if I were lighter.

I looked over my shoulder. He was gaining on me.

I looked ahead and saw my house come into view. It was going to be close.

As I ran for my life, the air going into my lungs felt like a hot knife. My heart was beating so fast, it felt like it would explode.

I hopped a fence with a single bound, like a giant scared rabbit. I was inside the boundary of my farm.

My door was getting closer. Just a few … more … steps.

I chanced a glance behind me and saw the wolf clear the fence with ease. He was right behind me. I wasn't sure I was going to make it.

I got to the door and shoved it open. I turned around and started pushing it shut, but before I could close it all the way, the wolf slammed his massive body into my door.

The force of the wolf slamming into the door popped my right shoulder. It felt like it was on fire. But, I could not let go of the door. If I let the pain stop me, I would become a meal for the wolf.

I took a deep breath and grunted as I pushed the door as hard as I could. I was almost there. Just a tiny bit more and ....

It was then that the wolf stood on its hind legs and sunk its sharp teeth into my left arm.

"AHHHHHHHHHH," I screamed. The pain was intense. The worst I had ever felt.

I reached over with my wounded hand and managed to grab a lit torch off the wall. I shoved the fire into the wolf's stomach, and he backed away just enough for me to close and lock the door.

After I locked the door, I sank to the floor. I could hear the wolf howling and hurtling its body against the door, trying to get in to devour me.

But, it was to no avail.

I don't know how long he kept at it, though, because I soon passed out from the pain.

Chapter 4

I have no idea how long I was unconscious. It seemed like a few hours at least.

When I came to, I heard banging on my door. At first, I thought it was the wolf.

I tried to stand up to look, but the pain in my arm made me stop. I looked down at the bite, and it was swollen and filled with pus. *Oh, gross!*

Through the haze of the pain, I thought I heard a voice.

"Steve," it seemed to say, "Steve, are you in there?"

"Who is that?" I croaked, my mouth as dry as sandpaper.

"Steve! Oh my goodness, you are alive," the voice said. "It's Ranger."

Ranger was one of the farmers in the nearby village. He was one of the few villagers I'd met who was a fair trader. When I first started my farm, he even helped me plant my crops.

"Ranger," I said, struggling to get to my feet. "Hold on and I'll open the door."

I unlocked the door and let him in.

"You look terrible," he said. "What happened?"

"A giant wolf attacked me."

"Here," he said, digging into a pocket in his brown robe and pulling out a bottle. "Drink this healing potion."

I tried to refuse. "Oh, I can't. It's too valuable."

"Nonsense. You are my friend. Drink it," he insisted.

I took the bottle from him, uncorked it, and drank. I could feel the magic of the potion start to work instantly. My hurt shoulder suddenly felt fine. More importantly, the swelling at the site of the wolf bite went away, but there was still an open wound.

"Wow," said Ranger. "I've never seen a bite that wasn't completely cured by a potion of healing. Must have been a bad bite."

I nodded. "Yeah, it really hurt."

"So," said Ranger, "how'd you end up with a wolf after you.

I explained everything to him and then added, "You know, I've been thinking. That wolf was probably twice the size of any other wolf I've seen. It was more vicious and more determined. There was something very odd about it."

"Probably some sort of old alpha male. Been wandering the forest for years. They are the most dangerous," said Ranger.

"Maybe," I replied. "But, it was almost like it was more than a wolf."

"What do you mean?" asked Ranger.

I rubbed my chin with my hand. "I'm not exactly sure."

Chapter 5

Ranger stayed with me for a few hours and helped me cook dinner. He left to return to his home before it got dark and the zombies came.

I was tired and went to sleep early, but I did not get much rest.

My dreams were filled with images of demons and monsters whose names I did not know.

In one dream, a strange child kept screaming at me, "WAKE UP! WAKE UP! WAKE UP!"

When I did wake up, I was covered with sweat and was shivering from fear.

I felt my forehead. I had a fever. *It could not be from the bite, could it? I drank a healing potion after all. The bite can't be infected.*

I got up and lit a torch and looked at the bite. It seemed as though it was starting to swell again.

I went to my sink and rinsed the bite mark with water. It felt good to wash it, but the wound felt sensitive.

I put the torch out and went back to bed.

As I lay in bed, I looked out my one window at the moon. It was bright tonight. Almost a full moon.

The moonbeams played across my body as I lay in bed. I looked at the strange shadows they made.

And, then, I looked at the bite mark again. What I saw petrified me.

It was glowing under the moonlight!

Chapter 6

The next morning, I felt much better. The bite mark seemed to be healing more, and I no longer had a fever.

After I ate some breakfast, I went outside and inspected the damage caused by the wolf. Apparently, after he had given up trying to get inside my house, he went to my chicken coop and ate all my chickens. He also knocked down part of a fence.

Stupid wolf, I thought.

I went back in the house and put on my armor and grabbed my sword and an axe. I needed to chop down some trees to get wood to repair the coop and the fence.

I feared the wolf might be near, so I stayed within sight of my house.

As I chopped down an oak tree, I noticed what appeared to be a sign in the ground in the distance. I'd never noticed a sign there before.

When I finished chopping down the tree, I walked over to the sign to investigate. The sign looked new. The wood from which it had been made was not weathered or faded.

But, that was not the curious part. The curious part was the writing on the sign. It said:

Moon, moon, make me swoon;
Get real big and I'm a loon.

What kind of nonsense is this? I thought. *Probably some villager playing a prank on me.* I shook my head and walked away from the sign, looking for another tree to cut down.

I soon came to a birch tree, which would be perfect for repairing my chicken coop. I quickly chopped it down and was about to return to my house when I noticed something in the distance.

It looked like a small pile of sand, which was completely out of place in this forest biome. I walked over investigate.

As I got closer, I saw it was a small pyramid, only three blocks high, made of sand.

What the heck?

I walked around the pyramid. When I got to the opposite side of the pyramid, there was another strange sign in the ground. This one said:

I like meat. It's a treat,
especially when it's people I eat.

I looked around quickly. I felt like someone must be playing a joke on me.

"Ranger? Ranger?" I called. "Is this you trying to be funny?" I got no response, and was not really expecting one. Ranger had better things to do than make suspicious signs all day long.

I shook my head and made my way back to my house quickly.

I spent the rest of the day repairing my fence and chicken coop. I wanted to make sure everything was secure.

Tonight would be a full moon, and it was easier for the hostile mobs to find things to attack and destroy.

I needed to be ready for anything.

Chapter 7

I was very tired by the end of the day. I had not worked that hard since the first day I spawned into the Overworld and had to build a house before dark.

I sat inside my house and cooked a pork chop and steak dinner. After I ate, I rested my sword next to my door and then lay down to go to sleep.

As I relaxed on top of my bed, waiting for sleep to take me, I looked out the window and saw that the moon was full. It was one of those huge moons; it looked like it was right next to the Earth.

I smiled at the glowing square. "At least some things in the world will always be nice," I muttered as I drifted to sleep.

***

That night I had a horrible dream.

The beams of moonlight hit the part of my arm where the wolf had bitten me, and I felt a searing pain. I sat up in bed screaming, but I did not awaken from my dream.

I looked down at my arm and it was swelling, filling with pus from the infection of the bite.

"AHHHHHHHHHH," I screamed as the pain intensified to an almost unbearable level.

I was panting for breath. Sucking in air between the shooting pains radiating from the bite mark on my left arm.

It hurt so bad in my dream, that I went to the door and picked up my sword. I raised the sword with my right hand and brought it down with all of my strength, hoping to cut off my own arm.

But, somehow, I missed my arm and the sword smashed into the door and it swung open.

Outside of the door stood someone who looked a lot like me, except he had glowing white eyes.

"Who are you?" I said through my teeth, clenching my jaw against the pain.

"I am your new master," he said flatly.

"Then help me with this pain," I screamed.

"Surrender yourself to it, Steve, and it will go away."

This guy was crazy. "I can't. It is too painful. I will die."

He laughed. "You will not die. I promise you."

"How can you make such a promise?" I yelled. "You have no idea how this feels."

At that moment, the gigantic wolf that had attacked me the other day seemingly appeared from nowhere and sat down next to the man with the glowing eyes.

"Make that creature go away," I begged.

The stranger with the glowing white eyes reached over and stroked the beast's head. "Why? He is perfectly well-mannered."

The pain in my arm was getting even stronger. I rubbed it with my right hand. It felt like it was on fire. The swelling had gotten worse.

"He had no manners last night when he attacked me!"

The stranger leveled his eerie glowing gaze at me. "He was simply following the bidding of his master," he said.

"What is your name, you freak?" I demanded.

"Why, don't you know?"

"No," I screamed. "Tell me."

"It is Herobrine."

As he said his name, a cold chill ran down my spine, even as the pain and the heat in my arm got worse.

I began to back away from the man, if a man he was, hoping to get back inside my house. As I backed away, I looked down at my arm and saw that it had sprouted thick black hair.

"What?" I said softly. "What is this?"

I looked from my arm to my hand and saw that my hand was now a paw with sharp claws.

I looked at the man with the glowing eyes. A wide, vicious smile was spreading across his face.

"What are you doing to me?" I said, panic starting to take over.

He never answered. Instead, he snapped his fingers, and the wolf leapt at my face. At the moment of impact, I woke from my dream, screaming.

Chapter 8

I was disoriented when I awoke. I swiveled my head around, checking my room. I wasn't sure at first that I was actually awake.

I looked down at my arm. No hair. No claw. No pain.

I could have sworn it was real, I thought. *But how could something so insane be real?*

I sat up, and swung my legs over the side of the bed. I sat there, with my feet on the floor, slumped over. I was rubbing the back of my head.

"Herobrine?" I said quietly. "What *was* he … or … it?"

I shook my head to clear the cobwebs from it. And then looked up and saw something that terrified me: my door was wide open, shattered into a bunch of pieces.

What? Had I really attacked the door with my sword in my dream?

I stood up and walked over to the door. The gouges in the door sure looked like they came from a sword and .... *Oh, no*, I thought, *are those claw marks?*

I took a few steps outside my door. Everything else seemed to be in order. My fence was still repaired, and my chicken coop was undamaged.

I had come to the conclusion that I just had a very bad dream and that I had been sleepwalking. Or, maybe I should say sleep-slicing. The claw marks must have been left over from the other night when the wolf attacked me.

I was just starting to clean up the pieces of the damaged door, when Ranger came running over the nearby hill. I had never seen him out here so early; it must be important.

Ranger ran up to me and took a few deep breaths before he started talking.

"Steve, the village was attacked last night," he said.

"Zombies?"

"No, Steve, something evil. A monstrosity." Ranger looked terrified. All of the blood had drained from his face. He was serious.

"What happened?" I asked, deeply concerned for my friend.

"It came out of nowhere. It tore two villagers in half with its claws. It ate some pigs. It even decapitated five zombies," said Ranger.

I put my hand to my mouth. "Oh my gosh. That sounds awful."

"It was," Ranger paused to gather himself, the emotional terror suddenly resurfacing. "It ... it looked like a wolf, only it could walk upright like a man. And ... it ... it ... had glowing white eyes."

I shivered. *Glowing white eyes? Had my dream been real? Or a vision of the future?*

"How did you manage to defeat it?"

"We didn't," said Ranger. "It left as quickly as it came. I have no idea why it decided to leave. But, we watched it run in the direction of your house, and we thought it might get you."

"I didn't see or hear anything," I said.

"You did not hear the howling?" asked Ranger.

"No."

"It was the most terrifying thing I have ever heard. It howled like a wolf possessed by a demon."

I shivered. After my dream last night, this was not something I needed to hear. "It sounds horrible," I said. "Would you like to come in and rest?"

Ranger nodded. "That would be nice," he said as he walked inside my house and sat down on the couch I had crafted from wood.

I picked up a few more pieces of the broken door and put them in a pile. Then I walked inside the house.

"Ranger, I – ," I stopped when I saw him. He was holding a bloodied piece of purple robe, with a giant claw slash across it.

Ranger was trembling. "One of the villagers killed was a priest. The creature slashed him with its claws and he bled to death."

"I don't know where that came from," I said sincerely.

"It was you?" said Ranger. "After all we did for you, you are the monster?"

"No, I did not do this. I was asleep all night," I said.

"It is not true," said Ranger, shaking his head sadly.

"Yes, Ranger, it is. I will prove it. I was having this weird dream about some man who came to visit me. He had glowing white eyes. Really creepy and –."

"Glowing white eyes?" said Ranger.

"Yes."

"Did he tell you his name was Herobrine?" asked Ranger, trembling.

How could he know? "Uh, yeah, he did."

Ranger rushed past me for the front door and ran to the gate in the fence. He turned around and yelled, "It *was* you. The demon

Herobrine has possessed you. You are now his pet monster. You are his werewolf!"

And with that, Ranger ran away to his village and left me terrified.

Chapter 9

The rest is fairly easy to explain.

Ranger and a few villagers came back the next day.

They gave me an ultimatum. Either leave the area or else build a strong dungeon into which they would lock me for the day before, the day of and the day after the full moon.

I liked Ranger, most of the villagers, and my farm. So, I spent the next three weeks mining stone and building a strong dungeon.

I gave the dungeon keys to Ranger.

It has held me for six full moons now.

But each night of the full moon, Herobrine appears to me in the dungeon along with his wolf. My bitten arm burns with pain, and the wolf attacks me immediately before I black out.

I have no idea what I do on those nights inside that lonely dungeon, but I always wake up exhausted with no memory.

I may be a slave to Herobrine's evil magic for one night every month, but I will not let him control me otherwise.

The End?

Can you help me?

Hey, guys, I hope you enjoyed reading these three diaries as much as I enjoyed writing them.

Just so you know, I'm busy working on more awesome Minecraft adventures for you to read.

In the meanwhile, please, *please*, **plz**, leave a review of this book where you bought it.

It's the best way for me to find out what you think about it. And, reviews really help out independent authors like me.

Thanks!

More Books

Do you want to know when the next unofficial Minecraft autobiography is coming out?

Then be sure to LIKE my Facebook page (facebook.com/drblockbooks) or follow my Instagram or Twitter (both @drblockbooks).

And, please check out the **first books** of my many Minecraft diary series:

Baby Zeke: Diary of a Chicken Jockey.

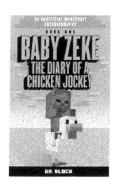

Diary of Herobrine: Book 1: Origins:

Diary of a Surfer Villager

About the Author

I, Dr. Block, believe that Minecraft is the greatest game ever created, mainly because it has the most awesome characters and mobs ever created.

I have been studying all the mobs and have worked with the most interesting of them to create and publish their autobiographies.

I am already working on more for you to read so you can learn about the amazing world that is Minecraft.

Stay tuned!